Disney

Aladdin
Trace 'n' Paint

A poor young boy Aladdin lives in the city of Agrabah.

His pet monkey Abu is always with him.

Jasmine is the daughter of the Sultan of Agrabah.
She stays in a grand palace.

This is Jasmine's father – the Sultan of Agrabah.

The evil Jafar is the Sultan's advisor.

Jasmine disguises herself and visits the marketplace.
There, she meets Aladdin.

Aladdin and Abu go to the Cave of Wonders.

They find a flying carpet and a magic lamp in the cave.
When Aladdin rubs the lamp, a Genie appears.

The Genie tells Aladdin that he can grant him three wishes
whenever he needs it.

The evil Jafar puts the Sultan under a spell and captures Jasmine. Using the Genie's three wishes, Aladdin defeats Jafar.

Jasmine and Aladdin decide to marry.